🌼 A GOLDEN BOOK • NEW YORK

Daddies copyright © 1953 by Random House LLC
We Help Daddy copyright © 1962 by Random House LLC
Animal Daddies and My Daddy copyright © 1968 by Random House LLC

All rights reserved. This 2015 edition was published in the United States by Golden Books, an imprint of Random House Children's Books, a division of Random House LLC, 1745 Broadway, New York, NY 10019, and in Canada by Random House of Canada Limited, Toronto, Penguin Random House Companies. The works that appear herein were originally published separately in 1953, 1962, and 1968. Golden Books, A Golden Book, A Little Golden Book, the G colophon, and the distinctive gold spine are registered trademarks of Random House LLC.

Visit us on the Web!
randomhouse.com/kids
Educators and librarians, for a variety of teaching tools, visit us at
RHTeachersLibrarians.com
Library of Congress Control Number: 2014930717
ISBN 978-0-553-49762-5
PRINTED IN CHINA
10 9 8 7 6 5 4 3 2 1

Daddies

By JANET FRANK • Illustrated by TIBOR GERGELY

What do Daddies do all day?
Daddies work while children play.

They work at desks.

They work in stores,

in factories

and out-of-doors.

Some Daddies help us keep well-fed.
They make buns and cakes and bread.

Some build planes.

Some make them fly.

Some catch fish for us to fry.

Dads make clocks

and Dads make chairs.

Farmer Dads grow corn and pears.

Dads are sailors dressed in blue.

And Daddies are policemen, too.

Dads dig coal

and Dads drive cars.

Dads put food in cans and jars.

Doctor Daddies keep folks well.

Daddies paint

and Daddies sell.

Daddies sit at desks and write

the books we read in bed each night.

Dads make steel

and Daddies sing.

Dads do almost everything.

But when they've worked the whole day through,
what do they like best to do?

By taxi, train, by car and bus,

Daddy rushes home—

to us!

We Help Daddy

By MINI STEIN • Illustrated by ELOISE WILKIN

We help Daddy a lot, Benjy and I. Daddy
fixes the attic door. He calls, "Hammer, please."

Benjy hands him the hammer.

Then Daddy says, "Sue, are you ready to help
me, too?"

I am Sue, so I hold out my hands to show
I am ready.

I bring the tin plate and Benjy puts the old
rusty nails in it.

"You are a help," Daddy says to us.

In the garden Daddy and Benjy pull out
weeds.

I pull out weeds, too. I see a nice little snail.
When he sees me, the snail puts his head in,
under his shell.

"Now we must water the plants," Daddy says.
Benjy turns on the faucet.
He helps Daddy water the big flowers.
I water the pink geranium with my very own
little watering can.

"The hedge needs a haircut," Daddy says.
Daddy picks up the shears and clip, clip,
clip—the hedge is neat and tidy.
Benjy gathers the clippings and throws them
in the waste basket. I help him.

Our dog, Zip, needs a bath. His paws are
muddy, and he has some burrs on his coat.
Zip does not like baths. He runs away. Benjy
and I catch him.

I wash his wiggly ears, Benjy soaps his curly coat. Daddy washes Zip all over.

Poor Zip looks so unhappy.

We splash warm water all over Zip and then
we rub him dry. Now Zip is nice and clean.

"The kitchen fence needs a coat of paint," says Daddy.

Benjy brings the paint brush. I spread newspaper so that Daddy can put the paint can on it.

We can see Mommy baking in the kitchen. She waves to us and says, "Hello, busy bees . . ."

Daddy dips the brush in the can and paints the rails.

I run and get my own little paint brush. Now I can help, too.

"We have a new picture to hang," calls Mommy.

We all go into the living room.

Benjy and I hold the picture up. Daddy puts wire cord through the two rings.

Daddy climbs the step ladder. I give him a hook to fix in the wall. Then up goes the picture.

"It's hanging all crooked," says Benjy.
Daddy straightens the picture and says,
"Thank you, Benjy."

Next we decide to make a bird feeder.
Daddy has a wooden tray for the bottom.
"I need two pieces for the sides," he says.
Benjy hands him the wood and Daddy
saws it in two.

I help Benjy keep hold while Daddy nails one piece of wood on each side of the tray. Then he nails the roof on and puts a big hook in it.

I put bread crumbs and seeds on the tray
and we hang it near the kitchen window. We
watch the birds eat.

"Let's get some logs for the fire," says Daddy.
Benjy and I push the wheelbarrow along.
Daddy chops the logs and we pile them in the
wheelbarrow and take them to the house.

Our next job is to clean the car. Daddy
takes the hose and splashes the car all over.
Benjy and Daddy wipe it dry.
I help, too.

"Hmm, we need to polish," says Daddy.

Daddy polishes the front. Benjy polishes the sides. I polish the door handles.

"See how the car shines," says Benjy.

"I'm glad I've got such good helpers," says Daddy with a smile.

Last of all we have to mend the handle on Benjy's dresser.

"Where's the screwdriver?" asks Daddy. Benjy finds the screwdriver for Daddy.

Daddy takes off the broken handle and screws on the new one.

"Thank you, Daddy," says Benjy.

"Wash your hands for supper," Mommy calls.

Benjy sees a nail sticking out of the bathroom door.

"That must come out before someone gets hurt," says Daddy.

"I'll get the pliers," says Benjy, and Daddy
pulls the nail out.

"What would I do without my helpers?" Daddy
says to Mommy.

After supper we are very, very sleepy. We had such a busy day helping Daddy.

Mommy tucks us into bed and says, "Daddy and I are so pleased with our two helpers."

Benjy and I are very pleased, too. Helping Daddy is fun!

ANIMAL DADDIES
and MY DADDY

By BARBARA SHOOK HAZEN

Illustrated by ILSE-MARGRET VOGEL

Beaver Daddy is a building Daddy.
He chews with his teeth.
He hammers with his tail.
He doesn't use a tool,
not even a nail.

My Daddy is a building Daddy, too,
but he uses many tools and glue.

Lion Daddy is fearless and brave.
He would do anything to save
his cub—if he had to.

My Daddy would, too.

Donkey Daddy is strong.
Just look at the load
he pulls down the road.

My Daddy is stronger.
He can pull
both Spot and me
up the hill.

Porcupine Daddy is a prickly Daddy.

The morning face of *my* Daddy tickles
before he shaves
and takes off his prickles.

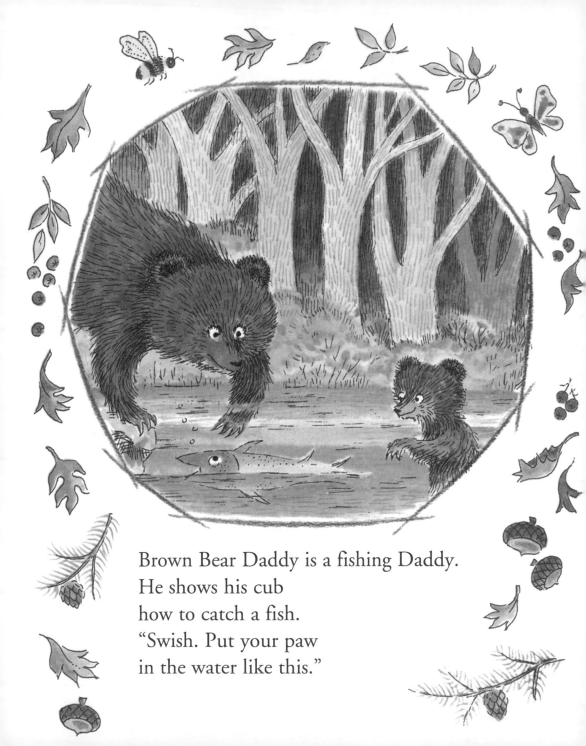

Brown Bear Daddy is a fishing Daddy.
He shows his cub
how to catch a fish.
"Swish. Put your paw
in the water like this."

My Daddy shows me
how to make a line
with a pole and a hook
and a ball of twine.

Daddy Giraffe is tall
as a tree.

My Daddy is tall.
Twice as tall
as all of me.

Mockingbird Daddy is a musical Daddy.
He serenades field and flower.
He sings to his family by the hour.

My Daddy
sings in the shower.

Polar Bear Daddy is a playful Daddy.
He loves to romp on the ice with his son.

My Daddy and I always have fun.

Elephant Daddy always has time.

So has *mine*.

Wolf Daddy is a watchful Daddy.
When Mother Wolf's gone
he guards the den.
He cares for the cubs
till she's home again.

On Saturdays Daddy sits with me
when Mother goes shopping with Aunt Bea.

Squirrel Daddy is a thrifty Daddy.

My Daddy saves.
One, two, three.
Three pennies in the bank for me.

Animal Daddies are all very fine.
But I'll take *my* Daddy any time.